THE SPACE-TIME PARADOX

A HAYWARD HALL SHORT STORY

ALEXANDRIA BLAELOCK

BlueMere Books
MELBOURNE, AUSTRALIA

For permission requests, please contact
enquiries@bluemerebooks.com.

Ordering Information:
Discounts are available on quantity purchases. For details, contact orders@bluemerebooks.com.

The Space-Time Paradox/Alexandria Blaelock
paperback ISBN: 978-1-925749-54-0
digital ISBN: 978-1-925749-55-7

Book Layout © BookDesignTemplates.com

THE SPACE-TIME PARADOX

It was Morag Clementine's first day at Hayward Hall, and so far, she was impressed.

Mystified, but impressed.

She'd arrived late in the afternoon.

There'd been some kind of mix up at the train station, and she'd wheeled her suitcase from the station along the hot, dry, featureless dusty road to the local village.

Fortunately, she was wearing jeans, a light shirt, and her sensible (and comfortable) lace-up brown brogues.

And fortunately, she'd been able to get a taxi up to the main house.

Silhouetted against the setting sun, Hayward Hall just looked wrong. The tiled roof, the feature brick patterns in the walls, the neat windows and imposing doors all looked perfectly fine when taken individually.

Yet somehow there was something not quite right about the overall impression of the house as a whole.

Some kind of blurry smudginess at the edges of her peripheral vision.

She rubbed her eyes and it went away.

The fountain was dry, the formal gardens overgrown, and creatures rustled in the undergrowth.

Hopefully not mice.

Not because she was afraid, but because they were devious little critters that were almost impossible to eliminate once they'd got a foothold.

The sound of rustling was almost obscured by the lorikeets screeching from the trees as they dipped and whirled from branch to branch, and tree to tree.

She'd turned to thank her driver, only to see the car driving away in a plume of dust. Perhaps a little too fast, or perhaps that was her imagination.

She'd looked once more at the Hall, expecting someone to walk out to welcome her, but the house remained as secure as if it had been shut up for decades.

Morag was a practical person, and as there didn't seem much point hanging around waiting for someone to come out, she opened the unlocked front door and went in.

Because to be honest it had been a long day, and she just wanted a cup of tea.

And funnily enough, given she'd been sitting in a train most of the day, she really wanted a sit down too.

Preferably in a cosy armchair.

Hayward Hall smelled of dust and cobwebs, and as she looked around the luxuriously ornamented foyer, she saw a lot of both. And almost immediately added dusting to her list of things to do.

It was cooler inside than out, and coming as she was from the Summer heat, she was grateful. And when the weather got even warmer, she expected she'd appreciate it even more.

The silent grandfather clock had stopped at fourteen minutes past nine, and she couldn't help but look at her watch to see the time was in fact twenty-seven minutes to eight.

Something else for the list.

"Hello," she called and listened for an answer.

There was no sound, and no movement, so she walked a little further in, knocked on the door labelled "Office," and called out again.

Still nothing.

When she opened the door, the displaced air sent clouds of dust into the air nearly choking her.

Clearly, the room hadn't been used to some time, so she closed the door, and spent a few minutes coughing.

She pulled her mobile phone from her pocket, intending to call the agency, but there were no bars and no reception.

She was starting to get annoyed.

Her contract was for a live-in housekeeper, so she walked through the dusty, cobweb festooned house to the back looking for the stairs down to the kitchen.

Ideally, before the light faded.

She left her suitcase by the stairs and descended.

"Hello?" she called as she entered the kitchen.

The basement was dim in the evening light, but with the aid of her phone's light, she was able to find the light switch.

Thankfully the kitchen was clean.

Spotlessly clean.

A modern, fully equipped catering kitchen with gleaming stainless-steel appliances and benchtops arranged around the walls.

She nodded with satisfaction as she noted juicers, mixers and coffee machine in amongst a jumble of other equipment that would need investigation.

At one end, a stove and cooktop, and at the other, an open door leading to the pantry and another for an office.

With what looked to be an exceedingly comfortable floral chintz armchair.

In the centre of the room, on an empty free-standing food preparation area, sat a conspicuous envelope.

On inspection, it contained three pages of spidery handwritten pages that Morag would need her glasses for.

She located the kettle, rinsed it out, filled it with fresh water and put it on to boil. She pulled a cup and saucer from the stacks next to the sink, rifled through the pantry to find tea and sugar, and looked in the fridge for milk.

Fully prepared now, she put her tea on the desk, adjusted the armchair so it was next to the desk, and pulled up a box to use as a footstool

With a sigh, she relaxed into the armchair, took a sip of tea and skimmed the letter.

- Apologies for not greeting her in person.
- Couldn't stay in the Hall a moment longer.
- Bedroom on the first floor, straight down the corridor, last on the left.
- The Young Master in the main bedroom at the front of the house.
- He's ill, don't bother him, unless he calls.
- Breakfast at 9am, Lunch at noon, afternoon tea at 4pm, dinner at 8pm.

Morag gently tapped the letter against her bottom lip.

By that schedule, the Young Master was due his dinner. Did the dinner requirement trump the do not disturb?

She didn't remember seeing any food plated up for his dinner.

She sighed, drank the last of her tea, and got up to check.

Definitely no dinner.

The only thing for it was to check what the Young Master wanted.

She stumped up the first flight of stairs to the ground floor, then collected her suitcase and stumped up the second flight to the first floor.

Took a detour to leave it in her room.

The bed was at least made, though whether it was with clean linen or not didn't matter as much.

She was so tired from her journey that when the time came, she would crawl in there and no doubt fall straight to sleep.

And she managed to find her way back to stand nervously at the Young Master's bedroom door.

Not quite so certain that interrupting him was the right thing to do, regardless of the circumstances.

The agency had told her she was not to bother him.

Likewise, the letter told her not to bother him.

Surely it would be fine.

Just this once. To introduce herself.

To enquire after his dinner needs.

She took a step back and away from the door, perhaps the last housekeeper had already prepared and delivered him a plate of dinner.

And done all the washing up and putting away afterwards.

It wasn't like she officially started work until the morning.

She was about to take another step back when she heard his voice through the door, "come."

Surprisingly deep and resonant.

With the title of the Young Master, she'd half expected a boy, though logically he must be at least 18 to be living in this big house on his own.

Well, not alone as such, but young boys required a different kind of housekeeper.

Someone who usually went with the title of Nanny.

The voice sounded more in the line of thirtyish if ever a voice could suggest an age.

Morag wiped her suddenly sweaty palms on her jeans and then smoothed down her hair.

It occurred to her that she was alone in a big house full of dust and cobwebs.

Where there was no mobile reception.

Perhaps it was wiser to keep backing away, and then run from the place as fast as she could. Just as the taxi driver and previous housekeeper had.

However.

The pay was insanely good, and the benefits weren't bad either.

She straightened her spine and pulled her shoulders back.

"I'm coming in," she said, just as much for her sake as for his, turned the knob and stepped through the doorway into a dining room.

A dining room comprising of small candlelit tables dressed in white cloths, with cutlery for at least four courses and wine glasses to match.

Which wasn't quite right, because this was supposed the be the Young Master's bedroom.

As she turned to check the door behind her, a couple walked past, looking quizzically at her.

Probably the same as she was looking at them given, they looked to be taking a break from filming something like a *Great Gatsby* adaptation, leaving a Hot Set behind them.

She refused to feel out of place in her jeans.

Morag could see through the open door behind her, to the corridor with its dirty pale blue carpet, yellow flocked wallpaper and an incredibly ugly brown waterscape of ducks flying over a pond.

And in the bedroom...

No.

In the dining room...

Walls of mirrors reflected the light from crystal chandeliers hanging from a painted, highly ornamented ceiling. Edwardian upholstered chairs in red matched the carpet and curtains.

Here and there, at other tables, there were more *Great Gatsby* extras. Eating. Drinking. Laughing.

Smoking.

She could still see the corridor she'd entered from, and when she peered around the frame to see the back of the door, there was no door at all. She was looking at the dining room.

She was about to walk back through the door, and close it behind her, when the surprisingly deep and resonant voice said, "Morag, don't be afraid."

"No, Young Master," she said, not turning away from the door, "why would I be afraid when your first-floor bedroom door leads into a hotel dining room? Clearly, I'm hallucinating, and need my rest more than you do."

"It's all right Morag. You're not hallucinating."

She snorted and turned to look at him.

His perfectly ordinary brown hair and eyes. Hands in the pant pockets of his perfectly ordinary Edwardian styled suit. His perfectly ordinary brown brogues.

His slightly smiling face.

"Is there really a hotel dining room in your bedroom then?"

"Not usually Morag," he shifted his weight from foot to foot, as if preparing to capture her, "though there's not always a bed either."

"Are you trying to hypnotise me, what with using my name all the time?"

He snorted, "not at all. I'm trying to sound soothing and reassuring so you won't run screaming out of the house."

"So, I'll ask you again, is there really a hotel inside your room?"

"Not as such," he pulled out a chair from the nearest table, "why don't you sit down and we can talk about it?"

She put her hands on her hips, "now you sound like you're trying to con me."

"What can I say to reassure you?"

"Can I leave the door open?"

"There's no need, but if it makes you feel more comfortable, then feel free."

She glanced back into the corridor.

There was no doubt wherever she was looked more attractive than the house. And wherever she was, looked like there was food and alcohol she didn't have to prepare herself.

Or do the dishes.

She shrugged and took the few steps to the table. He held the chair out as she sat, and helped her pull it in.

"So, where are we?"

He walked around the table to sit opposite her, "that depends on your perspective."

She frowned, or more realistically glared until he elaborated.

"We're still in the house, but this part of the house is now somewhere else."

"Where else?"

He looked around him, "at a guess, I'd say the Plaza Hotel, somewhere around 1910."

"That's quite a specific guess."

"Well, the Plaza opened in 1907, the new carpet smell has gone, and is showing a little wear."

She snorted, "how do you know it this is the Plaza, and that it opened in 1907?"

"I was here."

Morag opened her mouth. And then she shut it.

Again, she opened, and after a beat, closed her mouth.

There were too many questions related to those statements.

Then, "how could you have been at the Plaza, let's see..." she did a quick calculation, "111 years ago." She looked him up and down, "and about 80 years before you were born?"

He looked embarrassed, "let's just say there was an incident I'd really rather not go into right now. Can we talk about that later?"

She glared at him a little longer, and when he didn't seem inclined to say anything further, reluctantly nodded.

"Shall we have some dinner then?"

She nodded again.

He beckoned, and a tuxedo-clad waiter seemingly appeared from nowhere. He flicked a napkin open and lay it in her lap, and did the same for the Young Master.

The Young Master gave him a set of instructions in what seemed to be fluent French, so it seemed obvious they weren't in an Australian hotel.

The waiter nodded, removed some of the cutlery, and walked away.

Curious that his bedroom moved independently of the house in time *and* space.

Not that anyone would believe her.

She wouldn't have believed it herself except that she was sitting there, inside Hayward Hall. She checked behind her to see the door was still there.

And however unlikely, she was somewhere else as well.

"Paris?" she asked.

"New York."

"Can I go outside and see?"

"Best not without me." He checked his watch, "we only have a couple of hours here, and you can't be late."

"Young Master..." she growled a little in frustration, "must I keep calling you Young Master, or can I call you by your name?"

"Henry," he smiled, "my name is Henry Fox."

"So, Henry..."

The waiter brought a bottle of white wine, and she stopped talking to watch the proceedings. The waiter and showed Henry the label, and he nodded. The waiter removed the cork with a small pop and poured a little in the glass in front of Henry.

He swilled it around the glass, sniffed it, tasted it, then nodded. The waiter poured her a glass, topped up Henry's, then took the bottle away with him.

Morag sipped her wine, holding a little in her mouth to appreciate the crisp dry taste while the waiter cleared away the extra glasses.

"Henry—."

"Morag, I know you want answers, and I'd like to give them to you, but let's look at tonight as a kind of job interview.

"If I like you, you can stay. And if you like me, you can choose to stay.

"And in a day or two, if we agree you're to stay, then I will answer all your questions.

"Does that sound fair?"

However unfair that seemed, he'd effectively reminded her that he was her boss and not her date.

She shifted in her seat; of course, she didn't need to know anything more than he was prepared to tell her.

And of course, she wouldn't need to know anything unless he was employing her.

Feeling as though she was being put in her place, she nodded, "deal."

He smiled and held up his glass, "then, cheers."

She tapped it with hers, "cheers."

They drank.

And then sat in awkward silence.

Henry asked, "read any good books lately," at the same time Morag asked, "do you watch movies?"

They laughed for a moment, and he said, "go ahead."

"No, you go first."

"Ah, okay, well I was asking if you'd read any books."

She sipped her wine before she replied, "I'm not much of a reader at the moment, I'm usually too tired."

"Ah, that's a shame. I read the latest Epiphany Bombshell political thriller. It was intense."

"Was it? Perhaps you could lend it to me. If we agree on the contract, I won't be working nights anymore."

"I'll do that," he said.

"I usually watch movies," she said, "you tend to get more story in less time."

The waiter arrived, with two plates of shells covered in a green sauce, setting one before each of them. "Oysters Rockefeller," he said in heavily accented English, "*bon appétit*".

Morag bent to smell the dish before lifting a fork, "are you trying to wow me with your luxurious dinner then?"

He watched as she spooned one into her mouth, "not really. Oysters are common and cheap in this time."

"Oh, my goodness, that's good," she said, licking her lips.

He grunted in agreement but didn't stop to talk.

"Sorry," he said when he'd finished, "I didn't realise how hungry I was."

She was still trying to fork up the dressing that had spilt onto her plate, "umm, there's celery, and perhaps chives." She tutted for a moment, "capers, parsley, and some kind of alcohol." She smacked her lips, "I'm pretty sure I could approximate this."

"I'm sure you could. What were you saying?"

She frowned, "I've forgotten. No, wait, movies. I like books, but movies are quicker."

"What's your favourite then."

"I like fantasy and science fiction, but romantic comedies are easy to digest."

"Not mystery or suspense?"

"I'm not sure they're a thing these days, though I liked *Rear Window*."

The waiter returned to take the remains of the oysters away, along with the wine glasses.

Neither said anything.

The waiter came back with a bottle of red wine, letting Henry taste and approve the wine before he served it to her. Once more he left with the bottle.

She saluted him and sipped the rich, room temperature wine. "This is tasty. How do you come to know so much about wine?"

He sprawled a little in his seat, "in the old days when I was a child, Hayward Hall was always full of guests because my parents entertained a lot. It was quite a ways out of town in those days, and they had giant house parties. The wine stocks in Australia were quite limited so we travelled to Europe on buying expeditions. And then as time went by, my father wrote to the vineyards and replenished our stocks every year."

"May I know when that was?"

Henry looked at her for a while and was about to speak when the waiter arrived with the next course.

"Minted lamb, new potatoes and garden peas." He set the plates in front of them, and a small jug of gravy between them.

Morag held the edges of her seat, trying not to say or do anything that would distract him.

Henry picked up his fork and moved a few peas around the plate.

He sighed.

"1880."

Morag felt the floor falling away from her, and was glad she had a death grip on the seat.

"1880," she repeated. "Then you're at least... Twenty, twenty... 140 years old!"

He smiled a flat smile, "I was born in 1876, so 144 years to be exact."

"That's horrific!

"Damn it, that's not what I meant." She tried to think of a way to rephrase it to express exactly what she was feeling. "I mean, like," she waved her hands to suggest something more, "I'd go nuts being alive so long. How do you manage to keep going?"

He threw the wine down his throat, and beckoned for the waiter, "I don't have a choice."

Morag gulped her own wine, half horrified by the idea of living so long herself, half horrified for Henry's parents who had lost him to whatever hell he lived in, and half horrified that Henry had no one left who knew or cared about him.

That was too many halves for anyone.

They watched the waiter pour more wine into Henry's glass, and then hers, "leave it," he said, and the waiter backed away.

He savagely cut into his lamb and shovelled it into his mouth.

She watched and waited as he chewed.

"It's like that movie *Groundhog Day*," he said, cutting another slice of lamb, "except every day is different. I wake up, I walk out the door and start the day in another place and time.

"If I try to go back through the door into the house, I wake up the next day. If I die, I wake up the next day. If I stay up past midnight, I wake up the next day

"With whatever's the equivalent of the two quid I had in my pocket that last day in the house."

Morag took another gulp from her wineglass and clamped her spare hand between her thighs to stop herself from reaching out to him.

"That must be hard."

He grimaced, "like my mother used to say, what can't be cured, must be endured."

"But isn't there some way to fix this?"

"I'm not exactly sure what happened, so I don't know where to start fixing it."

"But with the resources of the universe at your disposal, you could go anywhere, and try anything!"

"For 24 hours only."

She scratched her head, then shook it.

What kind of sissy was he to live every day for a hundred years and not try to find a way out?

She did some more calculations in her head, "if you'd spent just two hours a day, every day, you'd have more than 60,000 hours worth of knowledge."

"I'm just trying to live a normal life, one day at a time, as best I can."

"So you haven't done anything, or learned anything that might be useful towards getting you out of here?"

"What's the point? It is what it is."

"And yet at least once, you tried to kill yourself to get out of here."

He sighed, and put down his cutlery, "I think you should go now. I think you should pack your suitcase and leave Hayward Hall."

"I—"

He stood up so abruptly his chair fell back on the carpet with a dull thud.

"You should leave."

"But—"

"GO."

And as she walked out the door, he slammed it behind her.

She tried to open it, but it wouldn't budge.

She looked at her watch; eleven o'clock.

Where had the time gone?

The house was in almost complete darkness, just a dim glow rising up the stairwell from the kitchen.

And the house was still, and utterly silent.

No rodents, no creaking as the house contracted in the cool evening air. No sign of owls, or possums, or other nocturnal creatures.

Morag was angry.

It seemed Henry had lost hope.

And she was defeated, fired before she'd even started, and with debts piling up.

She needed this job. It was the only thing the agency had offered her.

And she had no intention of leaving the Hall.

No intention of leaving him to his misery.

Her shoulders had ridden up without her noticing, so she forcibly dropped them.

She was here as a housekeeper, and keep the house was exactly what she planned to do.

Despite the skin crawling on the back of her neck, she didn't turn to look at the Master Bedroom come hotel dining room.

Just pulled out her phone, and used its light to guide her.

Turning the light on at the top of the stairs, she descended to the ground level and did a circuit of the rooms; shutting the front door, and making sure all the windows were secure before returning to the top floor to her bedroom.

She knew next to nothing about the incident that had sent flying in time and space, but she'd passed through a library, and a study, and chances were that the household records were kept in one or both of those.

And they were as good a place to start as any.

Back in her own room, she pulled out a journal to record her day. And as she started writing about Henry's dilemma, it occurred to her to wonder whether he kept records of his days.

He seemed to know a lot about the New York hotel, did he know as much about the other places he visited?

Perhaps there was some kind of pattern to when and where he landed.

If his pockets reset to two pounds every day, then if he kept a journal it would probably disappear every day. But if she was in the house...

Perhaps she could pass him a new journal each day, and maybe, just maybe the journal would appear in her room the next morning.

And perhaps it might not reset to a blank journal. Perhaps what he'd written that day would be there when she woke up in the morning?

And if it wasn't?

Maybe she could set up a mini-office outside his door and scan the records into a PC. And perhaps because they were in the house, they wouldn't disappear.

So the important thing for the morning was to explain her ideas to him and get him to at least try them out.

So where would he be in the morning?

And would it be a good place to start his research?

《《 • 》》

When she woke in the morning, she felt weirdly refreshed and raring to go. It might take a long time to do the research, and she wanted to get started as soon as possible.

But first, she had to make Henry breakfast and serve it at 9 am.

With no idea what he might want.

There was nothing in the pantry to suggest what he usually ate.

When she went on holidays, she usually tried to eat an enormous breakfast. Something that would keep her going perhaps as far as dinner. Though Henry's lunch was to be served at noon.

She made three bacon and egg rolls; two for Henry, and one for her. A thermos of coffee with two mugs, with a side of paper and a pen.

Standing before the door, she experienced a moment of nervousness but quashed it down.

He did not invite her to come in, so she boldly knocked on the door.

And after a few moments when he had not answered it, she knocked again, "Henry?"

Still nothing, so she opened it.

How interesting, he couldn't lock the door. He must have been standing with his back to it to hold it shut.

She allowed herself a grin as she looked onto a broad meadow filled with grasses and wildflowers, waving in a slight breeze. Birds called and swooped in the distance.

The day was on the cool side, and she wondered would he have warm enough clothes. That would make a grand experiment.

"Henry?" she called again, "Hello Henry?"

There was no reply.

"Henry, come out. I need to talk to you."

Still nothing.

"Will I take your breakfast away with me? It's bacon and egg rolls."

The sound of a body moving through the grass made her turn, though of course, she couldn't see through the door to the other side.

"Henry?"

He walked around the door, dressed as she was, in blue jeans and a blue striped t-shirt that were so nondescript they could have belonged any time in the last hundred years. And what looked to be the same brown brogues, "yes it's me. You said there something about bacon?"

It seemed ridiculous, but she asked anyway, "may I come in?"

And equally ridiculously, smiling at the idea, he gestured a welcome.

She stepped over the threshold, and offered the tray she was carrying towards him. He took a roll and started eating while she knelt, still holding the tray, and lay it on the ground.

"I hope you don't mind, I brought enough for two."

He nodded, and she poured two cups of sweet milky coffee before picking up her roll.

He sat, and they ate in a more or less companionable silence.

When he finished his first roll, he said, "I'm sorry for snapping at you last night."

"And I'm sorry for nagging you, I'm sure you've tried researching."

"I have, but you might have a new perspective, and I should at least hear you out," he picked up one of the coffees and took a sip.

"As a matter of fact," she said dusting off her hands and pickup up her coffee, "I do have an idea how we might progress the research."

"I'm all ears."

"Have you tried keeping a journal?"

"No."

She grinned, "I'd like to try an experiment, and this looks like a good day to try it out."

She outlined her ideas about the journal.

"It's not a bad plan. I've never woken up with anything other than the cash with me, but I've also never tried passing goods back and forth through the door. Let's do a couple of small-scale experiments now, and move on from there."

"What did you have in mind?"

He wrote something on a page, folded it into an aeroplane, and flew it through the door, "fetch," he said.

She rolled her eyes at him, and scrambled up and through the door. She unfolded the paper and showed him that the writing was still there.

"That's a positive sign," he said.

"Then I'll order the computer equipment," she said pulling out her phone and taking notes on it, "and see if I can get an express delivery—"

"What's that you have there?" Henry asked.

"My phone?" she looked blankly at him for a moment, "ah, you might not have understood them. It's kind of a machine, you can take notes, make phone calls, send texts."

"Can I see it?" he asked with an avaricious gleam in his eyes.

She dropped the paper back in the corridor and walked back to him. "I'm not sure it will work here," she said handing it over.

He turned it over and over in his hands, tapped a few buttons, and then dropped it in surprise when one of them was her music.

She scooped it up and turned it off.

"I think I want one of these too."

"It would certainly help, and I can order one for you, but I think maybe we should experiment with the paper first. In case it doesn't reset back to me."

"Sensible. But order one for me anyway, I can hand it back to you in the evening."

"Sure. Now, do you want me to bring you lunch at your usual time?"

"No, it's more important you get organised, and there's a town on the door side anyway." he reached into his pocket and counted out the contents, "and I have $120 at my disposal."

He looked at her, trying to gauge its adequacy.

"Sounds like you might be within a few decades of my time, and that ought to get you lunch with some left over."

"Fine," he said, getting to his feet, "meet you back here at 8?"

"Sure," she grinned at him, delighted that he was giving her the go-ahead, "in the meantime, why don't' you try to catalogue as much as you can remember of the last few days for me?"

"Okay," he squatted to fold the paper and pen into his pocket, then scooped up the last bacon roll.

"Ah. Keep the receipts for an expense claim against the estate accounts. Yvonne should have left some forms to sign giving you authority over the bank accounts, so once you've done that so you can use them."

"Cool," she said, shoving the phone into her back pocket.

He turned and started to walk away.

"Hey," she called out, "do you mind if I leave the tray here? To see what happens to it?"

He turned his head to look back at her, "sure. What's the worst that can happen?"

"Right," she said, dusting her hands together and turning towards him, "Now then. What was the date of the incident that started this?

"I'm not sure how that's relevant."

"Ah. I watched a show where some guy went travelling in time, and there was some kind of coinciding astrological and weather event."

He shrugged, "okay then, 9th of September 1904."

She made a note on her phone, "great, see you at dinner then!"

He waved and kept walking.

《《　•　》》

Back in the house, it seemed as though she ought to at least do a little light dusting. That was what she'd been employed for after all.

But making a start on the Henry Project seemed a better idea.

And more fun.

She called a cab and took a ride to the closest large shopping precinct.

First stop the bank to sort out the accounts and order a credit card - she had no idea how long it would be until she could get him out of there, and it would be much more convenient to order goods to be delivered than go out to get them.

Then she visited a computer store and paid over the odds to get laptops, printers and scanners shipped back to the house that afternoon.

She organised the phone and took that with her.

Then a bunch of notebooks and pens; a different colour for each day of the week. Thinking positively that if they used a book for each day of the week, any patterns would show up more easily.

Morag's footsteps slowed as she approached a Chinese restaurant, and smelled something tasty. She was so tempted to stop by for some tea and dumplings, but knowing she had a delivery due in a few hours made her speed up again.

But the lingering odour of chilli, garlic and onions was so delicious she turned around and ordered a serve of garlic chicken to take away.

Henry's plight was urgent, but she couldn't serve him well if she didn't take care of herself.

Back in the house, lunch consumed, she decided to set up the office because it had a fine view along the drive and the office was clearly next to the entry foyer for that reason.

Besides which, the household records were more likely to be in that space. And she might have time to look at some of them while she waited.

She looked in the ground floor store and retrieved an ancient barrel vacuum cleaner and some feather dusters that had stood the test of time.

More or less.

She opened the curtains, displacing more dust, and regretting her lack of a face mask.

Undeterred, she pulled her t-shirt up to cover her nose and opened the window as far as it would go.

The vacuum still worked, which made her wonder about the safety of the wiring, but it was heavy and difficult to manoeuvre.

Thank goodness she'd bought a surge protector and a backup battery to put between the computer equipment and the wall.

She swished the duster around in her left hand, and holding the suction pipe in her right, vacuumed the air first, and the curtains second.

She tried out the black Bakelite phone, and of course, it wasn't connected. She followed the lead back to the wall, to find the plug was like something she'd seen in a museum. That whole thing would need to be replaced.

She emptied the vacuum out the window, then vacuumed the carpet.

Which turned out to be blue with a yellow pattern that reminded her of the upstairs wallpaper. Had they commissioned carpet and wallpaper to match?

Hopefully, given the room was the only one with a phone line, and was located close to the front of the house, it would be easy to install a base station with handsets that would have sufficient range to get through the house.

She emptied the vacuum out the window once more, before returning the vacuum and dusters to the store, then filled a bucket with water and took it with some rags back to the office to wipe the surface down.

And wondered if she dared hire a squad of cleaners for a week or so and had the house thoroughly cleaned.

Would the house stand up to it?

Something to consider for another time.

With the office in a mostly usable condition, she went back upstairs to get her journal, then out into the garden to find a spot with phone coverage.

Which turned out to be right outside the door, so maybe it was just that the walls were old and thick, and well built.

Nonetheless, she'd need to get the internet connected up to the house, so she called her phone company and arranged a connection. The company had a cancellation and could come the next day.

She crossed her fingers that the power would be good enough for that too.

And then she sat in the shade of a tree and did some internet searches.

Within half an hour she'd discovered the 9th of September was indeed a good candidate for fantastical events:

- There had been a solar eclipse, and
- A low atmospheric pressure trough leading to unsettled weather, and

- An Antarctic disturbance had moved into the Bight.

All of which seemed an excellent indication that something significant had occurred on the day.

A little further investigation revealed the eclipse was part of two different series:

- The Saros cycle, next due the 25th of November 2030, and
- The Inex cycle, next due 31st May 2049.

Either of which was an unfortunately long time away.

Henry would surely be discouraged.

So that just meant that she had to keep him occupied with finding out how to reverse the effect.

And of course, time inside the Master Bedroom moved to its own drum.

And she'd be right outside, doing what she could to assist.

Or maybe she wouldn't tell him about the eclipses just yet.

Later that evening, washed and dressed in clean jeans and a long-sleeved shirt, she stood outside the door.

By this point, she'd hoped to have achieved a bit more.

But the laptop sat on a table she'd dragged from another room and set up on the corner of the wall, next to the door, partly blocking the corridor so she could take notes if she needed to. It was connected to a printer and a scanner in case she needed to make copies of anything.

Plus, she'd stacked all the journals and a bunch of other stationery in the hope that should it disappear during his night, it would reappear on the table.

Opposite the door, she'd set up an incident board, like you see in crime shows, where she could keep him up to date on her investigations. Currently showing the page he'd given her that morning.

She'd set up an email account for him, and downloaded a bunch of apps that might be useful to his phone. The hard part might be teaching him how to use the phone.

She rolled her neck against her shoulders, then linked her fingers together, turning her palms outward, and stretched side to side, forward and backwards, and knocked on the door before she was ready.

He opened it just as she was turning away to stretch her back.

"You're back!" he said.

She turned back to face him, "my front!" she said, and he snorted.

He was inside a pub.

"Ah, so the door turns up wherever you are," she said, "that's good to know."

He grinned and stood back so she could see.

It might have been a themed pub, or it might have been an actual British pub.

It wasn't that different to one she'd visited in London called the Nag's Head, with worn wooden floors, chipped and dented tables and chairs, and of course darts boards at the end of the bar.

The air was fragrant with beer, steak and chips, and a hint of mayonnaise. The sound of muted conversation suggested the pub was half full.

She stepped back to show him her incident room styling, hoping it would look suitably futuristic and full of potential.

He seemed suitably impressed, but he could tell something about her was off.

"Look," he said, "come in and we'll order, then you can tell me what's bugging you."

She chose steak and chips with salad and beer, and Henry ordered the same. They took a number and brought it back to their table.

The beer when it arrived was warm, which if nothing else confirmed the geographical exactness of the British pub.

"So, what's up?"

She pulled out her journal and looked at his hopeful, yet puzzled face.

She couldn't lie to him.

So, she relayed the findings of the day's researches.

He surprised her, "that's fantastic! This is great news - you're hired!"

She looked at his radiant face, wondering if he'd finally gone mad.

"I'm sorry? I'm hired?"

He took a swig of his beer, and nudged hers closer to her, "yes, you're hired."

"I'm hired?" she repeated, "I don't understand."

He grinned, "24 hours ago I was telling you to get lost. I didn't know anything about the situation I find myself in. And today I know there may have been two sets of cosmic influences."

"But it might be decades before you can live a normal life."

"Ah, but I live in a time machine, and if you take the job, I've got you on the outside."

"But I haven't done anything that no one else could do."

A cheerful waitress came through and left their meals, and after being reassured they weren't expecting anything else, taking the number away with her.

He picked a chip off his plate, sucking the air through his mouth to cool it before he could chew it.

"No one bothered until you."

She speared a bit of salad and chewed.

It was true she needed a job. And this was the kind of job could make a significant difference in the life of her employer.

Furthermore, her new boss wouldn't be under her feet micromanaging all day.

"All right, I'll take it."

He jumped up and gave her a spontaneous kiss on each cheek, "that's the best news I've heard since five minutes ago!"

《 《 • 》 》

It was the November 25 2030, and Morag'd been working at Hayward Hall for almost a decade.

She stood outside the Master Bedroom door, listening intently to the sounds within.

If their calculations were correct, at 11:57 she would be able to enter the Master Bedroom at the time Henry had detonated the device that sent him spinning through space and time.

She stood, her eyes fastened on the GPS linked watch on her left wrist showing the exact time, and the other hand on the doorknob.

Counting down.

Henry had described the situation, so she knew what she was looking for.

At exactly 11:57, she threw the door open, sprinted across the bedroom and slapped the device from his hand.

"What the devil do you think you're doing?" he demanded.

"I'm saving you from yourself."

The device detonated with a flash, and she covered him from the fallout with her body.

The light got brighter and brighter, and she had to close her eyes against the glare.

But she was jubilant. She had saved him.

She would wake up the next morning in her bed, and he would wake in his.

Job done.

THE END

ABOUT THE AUTHOR

Alexandria Blaelock writes stories, some of them for *Ellery Queen's Mystery Magazine* and *Pulphouse Fiction Magazine*. She's also written four self-help books applying business techniques to personal matters like getting dressed, cleaning house, and feeding your friends.

As a recovering Project Manager, she's probably too fond of sticking to plan. She lives in a forest because she enjoys birdsong, the scent of gum leaves and the sun on her face. When not telecommuting to parallel universes from her Melbourne based imagination, she watches K-dramas, talks to animals, and drinks Campari. At the same time.

Discover more at www.alexandriablaelock.com.

BOOKS BY
ALEXANDRIA BLAELOCK

SHORT STORY COLLECTIONS

The Histories of Hayward Hall
Lovelorn, Lovestruck and Love at First Sight
Common or Garden Variety Heroes
Case Files of the Wilkinson Detective Agency
Unavoidable Fates

OTHER FICTION

That Love Nonsense

MS BLAELOCK'S BOOKS

Stress Free Dinner Parties
Signature Wardrobe Planning
Holistic Personal Finance
Minimally Viable Housekeeping
Planning a Life Worth Living